The Buried Moon
and other stories

The Buried Moon
and other stories

selected and illustrated by **Molly Bang**

CHARLES SCRIBNER'S SONS · NEW YORK

"William and Jack and the King of England" is from
A Dictionary of British Folktales, Part A, Folk Narratives, Vol. 1,
edited by Katharine M. Briggs. Copyright © 1970 by K. M. Briggs.
Reprinted by permission of Indiana University Press.

"The Mad Priest" is from *Strange Stories from a Chinese Studio*,
translated by Herbert A. Giles, published by Kelly and Walsh, Ltd.

Library of Congress Cataloging in Publication Data
Main entry under title:
The buried moon and other stories.
SUMMARY: A collection of five folk tales from
various countries about the feelings buried deep within us.
1. Tales. [1. Folklore] I. Bang, Molly.
PZ8.1.B8757   398.2'7   76-58328
ISBN 0-684-14666-5

1 3 5 7 9 11 13 15 17 19 MD/C 20 18 16 14 12 10 8 6 4 2

Printed in the United States of America

Contents

To our own moon
and sun
and daughter
MONIKA

Preface

This collection was originally intended to be a sequel to
The Goblins Giggle — a group of scary stories which all
ended happily. As the stories were found, discarded, and
selected out, I found myself less drawn to scary stories
per se as to those which seemed deeper, more meaning-
ful. These five were finally decided on. "The Buried
Moon" is a tale from England, as is "William and Jack and
the King of England.""Savitri and the Lord of the Dead"
is from the Indian epic *Mahabharata* and is known to
every Indian child. "The Mad Priest," a goofy story I have
long loved, is from *Strange Tales from a Chinese Studio*,
a collection of three hundred stories written by a man
who was fired from his post in the Chinese government
several centuries ago. "The Wolf in Disguise" is an
amalgam of the Grimm *Wolf and the Seven Kids* and a
Japanese version of the same tale.

In the order presented here, the stories depict the

progress of human life, from birth, or "rebirth," through adventure away from home, adult responsibility and dedication, to retirement from society for a spiritual life alone in nature. The last tale concerns the Nature which protects us and which we must protect in turn.

At the same time, these are stories of the buried moon inside us all, which only experience, effort, and trust will enable us to find and set free.

— Molly Bang

The Wolf in Disguise

There once was a poor widow who had three children: a girl, a boy, and a little baby. One day she had to go far across the moor to market, so she called the two older children and warned them, "There is a wolf on the moor who eats up little children. While I am away, take care of the baby, and let no one into the house."

She kissed them all good-bye and went away over the moor.

Some time later, the wolf came to the house, disguised as the mother. He stood outside the door and called out,

> *Children dear, your mother is here,*
> *Back from the market, back from the moor.*
> *The sun is high; my throat is dry.*
> *Unbolt the latch and open the door.*

But the wolf's voice was loud and gruff and deep. The girl called back,

Our mother's voice is clear and sweet,
Like sweetest honey from the moor.
Your voice is loud and gruff and deep.
You're the wolf! We won't unbolt the door.

The wolf ran to the grocer's. He bought some honey and drank it down. Then he returned to the house, and in a clear sweet voice he called out,

Children dear, your mother is here,
Back from the market, back from the moor.
The sun is down; my feet are worn.
Unbolt the latch and open the door.

Though the wolf's voice sounded just like their mother's, he put his hairy black paws against the window as he spoke. The boy saw them and called back,

Our mother's hands are soft and white,
Like mallow flowers on the moor.
Your hands are hairy and black as night.
You're the wolf! We won't unbolt the door.

So the wolf went off and shaved his paws and then ran to the miller's and asked for some flour. He rubbed the flour on his paws until they were white and returned to the house once more. By this time it was quite dark.

The wolf stood at the door and called out,

Children dear, your mother is here,
Back from the market, back from the moor.
The sun is gone, but I am home.
Unbolt the latch and open the door.

But the children still were not sure it was their mother, so they asked her to put her hands through the window. The wolf put his paws through the window, and indeed they were soft and white, just like their mother's. So the children opened the door, and in walked the wolf, all dressed like their mother. The wolf sent the two older children to bed and then went into the other room with the baby. As the baby slept, the wolf gobbled it up. Then he took off his clothes and lay down to sleep, planning to eat the other children when he woke up.

In the middle of the night, the boy got up to get a drink of water. As he passed by the other room, what should he see in the moonlight but a wolf with white paws asleep on his mother's bed! The boy ran to his sister and woke her up. She took a bottle full of oil from the kitchen and the two children crept out of the house. They ran out the gate and climbed the tree by the pond, and poured the oil all around the trunk below them.

When the wolf woke up and found the children gone, he ran out after them, through the gate and over to the pond. When he looked into the water, there were the reflections of the boy and the girl looking up at him.

"Now I've got you!" he cried with glee, and he jumped right into the pond! But the children, of course, were up in the tree, and all the wolf found in the water were frogs. He crawled out of the pond and shook himself off, and he saw the children above him.

"Now I've got you indeed!" he said, and he began to climb up the tree.

But the oil made the tree too slippery to hold onto, and time after time the wolf slid back down to the ground. At last he thought of an idea. He licked the oil off the tree trunk, and when the oil was all gone, he climbed up the tree and ate the children up. Then he climbed back down and fell asleep.

The day had just dawned when the children's mother returned. She saw the open gate and the open door and the wolf lying asleep at the foot of the tree, and she understood what had happened. She was so sad that she could only stand on the path and stare at the sleeping wolf.

As she looked at him, she thought she saw something move inside his stomach, and she wondered, "Oh, could my dear children still be alive?"

She took out scissors from her bag and cut open the wolf's stomach. One after the other her children crawled out; last of all came the baby. They were alive and well as could be, for the wolf had swallowed them whole. They hugged their mother and rejoiced, but she told them to run quickly and find some stones. Quiet as could be, she piled the stones into the wolf's stomach until it was full, and she sewed it back up. Then the four of them went back inside the house and bolted the door.

When the wolf awoke, he was very thirsty, so he got up and walked to the pond. His stomach felt very, very heavy, and the stones inside knocked against each other as he walked. The wolf said to himself,

> *What rumbles and tumbles*
> *Against my poor bones?*
> *Those three little children*
> *Are heavy as stones.*

When the wolf reached the pond and leaned over to take a drink, his foot slipped on the bank and he fell into the water and drowned. That was the end of the wolf on the moor. The children danced for joy and their mother made them all new clothes from the dress the wolf had left behind.

William and Jack
and the King of England

There were once an old man and an old woman who lived on the side of a mountain. They had two sons named William and Jack, who were as alike as two berries and who loved each other as much as they loved themselves. When William grew old enough, he decided it was time for him to seek his fortune, so he said to his mother,

"Roast me a collop and bake me a bannock, and I'll be off to seek my fortune."

"Will you take a wee bannock with my blessing," she asked him, "or will you take a big bannock with my curse?"

"I'll take the big bannock," said William, so his mother gave him the big bannock and her curse.

Before he left, William called his brother Jack into the garden, where he had planted a bush, and said, "If this bush stays green you'll know I am well, but if it withers, you'll know I am ill and need your help."

So William set out, and he went on and on, farther than he had known there was. There was rest for the birds in the branches of trees, rest for the beasts in holes underground, and rest for the fishes in water-weeds, but there was no rest for poor William. He went on through the night, and in the darkness he stumbled and fell down a precipice.

As he
fell, William
thought he saw a light
in the cliff across the way,
so he got up and walked until he
found a footpath up the cliff, and he
climbed it until he came to a wee house
where there was an old, old man who sat
roasting a sheep. He was a fearsome-looking
man, but he divided the sheep with William and let
him spend the night there. Yet the man looked so fear-some that William was afraid, and as soon as the old man fell asleep, he crept out of the house and went on.

He traveled on and on until he saw a castle in the distance. At the castle gates there was a lodge. An old woman came to the door and let him in; she said that she and her daughter were so poor they only had birds' feet to eat, but he could share the poor fare with them. When William went inside, he found that the old woman had a pretty daughter. William had never seen a girl in his life, and he was much taken by her, and she was much taken by him. The witch (for that is who she was) and her daughter tried to make William stay with them, but he wanted to go to the castle.

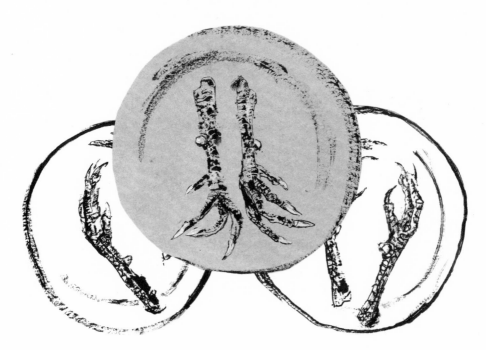

"The king is a savage man," said the witch, "and he will set impossible tasks for you to do." But William would not be dissuaded from going. He knocked at the castle gates and asked the servants if the king had work for him to do. When the servants asked the king if there was work to be done he replied, "Let the stranger clean the nine-stalled stables."

The servants gave the king's answer to William, but they warned him, "The horses are savage and will kill you. No one has dared to go near them for years."

William went to the nine-stalled stables and pushed the doors, but the doors were stuck fast with years of dung and would not open. William climbed onto the stable roof and let himself down through the skylight, and he found that the stables were full of horse dung. He found a spade and pitchfork and began to clean out the stables. One whole week he shoveled, then two, then three, and by the end of the third week he had cleaned them all out.

When he was not shoveling, he took care of the horses. He fed them and watered them and rubbed them down, and he thought to himself,

"This is no way to keep beautiful horses like these. No wonder they were so savage." The horses were not savage to him at all, and he had no trouble with them.

William washed himself, and then he looked over

the harnesses which hung on the wall of the stables. They were old and black with age, so William took them outside to clean them. He cleaned them and polished them, when lo and behold they shone in the sun and he saw that they were mounted in pure gold.

He sat there outside the stables polishing the gold-mounted harnesses when the princess passed by. She thought he was the handsomest man she had ever seen. The princess went home and suddenly took to her bed.

The king sent for all the doctors in the land, but no one could discover what had made her ill until there came to the palace an old Scottish doctor.

"I must see the princess alone," he said.

When the doctor was alone with the princess, he talked with her for a while and then he said,

"I know what is the matter with you; you are in love."

"That must be it," said the princess, and the doctor went and told the king.

The king came to ask his daughter about this and she told him,

"I am in love with your groom of the nine-stalled stables."

"Mercy!" said the king. "Is that stranger still alive then? I thought he must have been killed long ago." And he went to the stables to see the groom. When the king saw William sitting there, he said to himself,

"I don't blame my daughter. Had I been a woman, I would have fallen in love with him myself."

The king and his councillors told William that the princess was in love with him, and that he should marry her if he wanted to save her life. William was very surprised, but he got up and went to the princess where she lay in bed, and he said to her,

"I'm sorry you are ill, and I'll marry you if it will save your life."

The princess was cured at once, and she got up out of bed. There was a royal wedding, and after the wedding a royal banquet, and after the banquet a wedding dance. William danced with all the ladies, and he danced with the daughter of the witch who lived at the lodge at the castle gates. The daughter was jealous that William had married the princess instead of herself, and she stuck an enchanted thorn behind his ear while she danced with him.

When the thorn pierced his skin, William fell to the floor like one struck dead. The king, the courtiers, the guests, and the doctors all saw that William was dead, and they made preparations to bury him. But the princess refused to let him be put in the ground. She had him placed in a coffin of lead, and had the coffin carried to the topmost room of the castle, where she sat with him and looked at him day after day.

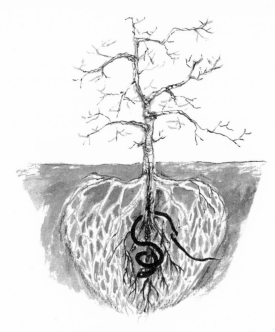

Back on the mountain, Jack was walking in the garden one day when he saw that William's bush had withered, and he knew that his brother was ill and his life was in peril.

Jack went to his mother and said,

"Bake me a bannock and roast me a collop, and I'll set out to seek my brother." His mother and father tried to persuade him to stay, but he would not, so his mother said to him,

"Will you have a wee bannock with my blessing, or a big bannock with my curse?"

"I'll have the wee bannock," said Jack, and so he got the wee bannock and his mother's blessing, and he set out after his brother.

He followed the same road as William had done, and he went on and on, farther than he had known there was. There was rest for the birds in the branches of trees, rest for the beasts in holes underground, and rest for the fishes in waterweeds, but there was no rest for poor Jack. He went on through the night, and in the darkness he fell down the precipice, and saw the light, and climbed the cliff, and found the wee house.

When the old man saw Jack, he said, "What have you done with yourself all this while?" So Jack knew his brother had been this way before him, and he answered, "I went outside and lost my way."

"Well," said the old man, "stay with me for a while and I'll teach you swordplay." Jack did not mind the man's fearsome looks, and he stayed a month with him and learned all there was to know about swordplay.

He left the old man and went on and on, until he came to the lodge at the castle gates. He knocked at the door and the daughter got up from her supper and answered. When she saw Jack standing there she let out a shriek. "A ghost! A ghost!" she screamed. "He's come back to get me!" She and her mother fled out the door and were never seen again.

Jack guessed that they had had something to do with his brother's fate. He walked into the house and finished the meal on the table and took a purse with seven gold pieces in it. Then he went and knocked at the gates of the castle. When the gatekeeper answered it, he too thought Jack was the ghost of his dead brother, and he fled. Jack walked up to the castle and knocked on the door, but when the butler answered and found him there, he ran back to the servants' hall and told all the servants that the ghost of dead William was standing at the door.

The cook stood up and said, "I never hurt him dead or alive, and he'll never hurt me." She took the Bible under her arm and went to speak with the stranger. Jack told her who he was, and he asked to see his brother's body.

The servants were afraid to take him, but he gave them the seven pieces of gold, and they took him up to the topmost room.

The princess wasn't there, so Jack opened the coffin and took his brother out. As he held William's head, he found the thorn of sleep behind his ear and pulled it out. William at once sat up and rubbed his eyes. Just then the princess walked into the room, and when she saw Jack she thought it was William, and she ran to him and kissed him. But when she saw William, she was very confused. After the princess came the king, and he shook hands with Jack and told him he was glad to see him alive, but then he too saw William and didn't know what to do.

Jack explained what had happened, and the rejoicing lasted for many days. Jack wanted to leave the castle
at once, so he could go out and seek his own fortune and
return with it to his mother and father, but William and
the princess begged him to stay until a baby boy was
born.

So Jack stayed on for nine months more, when the
princess gave birth to a little prince. The princess asked
Jack to stay just a few days more, until she had baked him
seven bannocks. She mixed the bannocks with the milk
from her own breast and gave them to Jack, saying,

"When you meet your enemy, give him these and say
to him, 'Taste of my bread.'"

William gave him a magic sword, and Jack set out at
last. He walked and walked until he came to a green hill,
where he sat down to rest. Jack looked below him and
saw an avenue of trees with an old deserted road running
between them. He walked down to the road and came to
a gate, and he said aloud, "I'll stay on this road."

Then a voice behind him said, "You'll not stay on this
road." Jack turned and saw a little man with a sword in his
hand, and a millwheel for a hat, who said,

"I catch everything, man, bird, or beast that comes
this way. This is the Forbidden Land, and now I'll catch
you."

"We'll see about that," said Jack, and they had a

terrible fight. In the end Jack struck the sword out of the little man's hand. The little man said,

"That's my sword you're fighting me with or you'd never have beaten me. Now I am beaten and I will give you these two things."

The man opened a sack at his belt and took out a ragged coat and a pair of worn old shoes.

"This is the cloak of invisibility and these are the shoes of swiftness," he said. "Perhaps some day you will have need of them."

Jack took the cloak and the shoes and walked on down the avenue lined with trees. After many days he came to another country, where he saw ahead of him an old man cutting rushes. Jack decided to try out the cloak, so he put it on and walked up to the man.

"Good morning, sir," he said. The man stood up and looked all about him. "Who said that?" he asked. "Where are you?"

"Right here in front of you," said Jack. The old man could see nothing at all, and he was frightened out of his wits, when Jack took off the cloak and said,

"Do you see me now?"

"Yes, I see you now," he said. "Why didn't I see you before?"

Jack explained to him about the cloak and the shoes, and the man said,

"I've been cutting rushes here for two hundred years, and I've never seen the likes of that before. But you had better watch out. One day, every seven years, the Black Knight comes here to try to catch his daughter, who turned into a milk-white deer to escape his evil magic. The seven years will soon be up and he'll kill anyone who stands in his way."

"Maybe I'll catch the deer first," said Jack.

"It would be a blessing if you do," said the man, "for

you would free us all from the power of the Black Knight."

Jack put on the shoes of swiftness and off he went to look for the milk-white deer. He saw it far off in the distance and made after it, but it was fleet of foot and knew the terrain well. Jack put on his cloak of invisibility, and the deer thought she had escaped him, so she slowed her pace and went on until she came to a rocky precipice. Jack followed behind her unseen, and he thought he had her cornered when suddenly the rock opened and the deer walked inside. Jack ran in after her and the rock wall closed behind him.

The deer lay on the ground panting, and Jack took off his cloak and appeared before her as clear as day.

"I have you at last, my lady," he said.

The deer was startled.

"Aye, you have me," she said, "and there's one thing for you to do. Do you see that well over there? You must cut my head off my body and fling them both down into that well."

"But I don't want to hurt you, you pretty creature," said Jack.

"There's no help for it," said the deer. "And if you don't I'll cut your head off instead."

"I wouldn't want you to do that," said Jack. So he cut

off her head and flung the head and body down into the well. Then he thought to himself,

"What a fool I was! The wee deer could never have taken my sword in its foot. What a fool I was to believe it! Why did I hurt the wee deer?"

But as he sat and grieved, he heard a voice behind him say,

"Look up, Jack."

And there was a most lovely lady.

"I am the milk-white deer," she said. "And now let us go home."

The princess spoke a magic word and the rock which had closed behind them opened once again, and there was a road and a grand carriage on it, and Jack and the lady climbed in. The carriage drove on, but it had not gone far before they saw a horseman riding toward them, and the princess said,

"This is my father, the Black Knight. He is the deadliest man on the face of the earth, and I fear he will kill you."

The Black Knight rode up to them, drawing his sword. Jack jumped down from the carriage and drew his own, but before he began to fight, he remembered the seven bannocks the princess had baked for him and he took them out.

"Taste of my bread," he said to the Black Knight, and he held the bannocks out to him. The Black Knight took one bite, and his face changed. He ate all the seven bannocks, and when he had finished he was the sweetest and gentlest man in all the world.

"Thank you, Jack," he said. "You have done for me what no other earthly man could have done, and you have freed my daughter from enchantment."

So Jack and the princess were married, and they lived with Jack's mother and father and the Black Knight in the kingdom beside his brother William's.

Savitri and the Lord
of the Dead

There was once a king named Aswapati. He was virtuous and pious, and he ruled so well that he was beloved by townspeople and farmers alike. But the king grew old. Still he had no children, and he was full of grief at this.

In hopes of having children, the king left the palace to live alone. He ate simple food, wore simple clothes, and observed strict vows. Every day he lit a fire and offered prayers to the goddess Savitri. He continued in this way for eighteen years, when at last one day the goddess appeared to him in the flames and said,

"I am pleased, O king, with thy prayers, thy fasting, and thy virtue. Know then, mighty Aswapati, that a daughter of great energy will soon be born to you."

The goddess vanished, and the king returned to his palace and resumed his duties. Soon a daughter was born to his queen, and in gratitude to the goddess they named the child Savitri. The girl grew into a young woman, with golden skin and eyes like lotus petals. People who saw her thought that a goddess had come down to earth. But there was no man who could match her in energy or virtue or splendor, and no one asked for her in marriage.

Aswapati said to her one day,

"It is time for you to be married, yet no one asks for your hand. You then, Savitri, go seek a husband who is equal to yourself in quality."

Savitri left her father and mother. She set out in a royal caravan, accompanied by servants and councillors, and she traveled to holy places throughout the country, where she talked with ascetics and distributed wealth.

It was many months later, while her father Aswapati was in his court talking with the holy man Narada, that Savitri returned. The king greeted her with joy and asked her if she had decided who was to be her husband. Savitri replied,

"Father, there was a virtuous king of the Salwas people named Dumatsena, who after many years of wise rule became blind. An enemy learned of the king's misfortune and invaded the country, and the king was forced to flee into the woods with his wife and their infant son. The royal family lived in great poverty and simplicity, while the boy grew to manhood. We came upon him as he was entering the forest to cut wood for his parents.

That man I have accepted in my heart and it is he whom I will marry."

All the while Savitri spoke, the holy man Narada grew more and more anxious, and when she had finished he said to the king,

"Sire, your daughter has chosen wrongly. The name of the youth she saw is Satyavan. He has the energy of the sun, the courage of the gods, and is as forgiving as the earth itself. He is truthful and generous, and as handsome as the moon."

"You tell that he has every virtue, and yet you say that Savitri has chosen wrongly. What then are his defects?" the king asked.

Narada replied, "He has only one defect and no other, but it is strong enough to cancel all his virtues. Twelve months from this very day, Satyavan is destined to die. If you marry this man, Savitri, you will be a widow within the year."

The king turned sadly to his daughter and said,

"You have heard the words of Narada. Go out again and choose another."

But Savitri replied, "As death comes but once, so can I give my heart only once. I have chosen, and now I must face whatever comes to my husband."

Narada and the king marveled at the steadfastness of her heart, and they approved her decision. The next day King Aswapati traveled to the woods where the royal family lived and asked for their son in marriage to his daughter. The king and queen accepted and asked only that Savitri come and live with them, instead of taking their son to live with her family, as was the custom. So Savitri and Satyavan were married, and Savitri put away her royal robes and her jewels and went to the forest to live.

The weeks turned to months, and the family grew to love one another. But Savitri remembered the words of Narada, and she counted the days that numbered her husband's life. She saw by the attitude of the king and queen that she alone knew of Satyavan's approaching death, and she kept the knowledge to herself.

Four days before the appointed time, Savitri took a vow. She would neither eat nor sleep for three days and nights, and would spend the time in watchfulness and prayer. In this way she hoped to achieve a state of mind that would allow her to see and hear things that are unknown to most mortals.

The king and queen could not understand the reason for her fast, and they begged her to eat, to sleep. But Savitri said to them, "I have taken a vow," and they could say no more.

When the morning of the fourth day dawned, Savitri still would not eat.

"I will eat when the sun sets," she said. "Mother, father, I have never asked you for anything before, but today I cannot bear to be parted from my husband. May I go into the woods and stay with him the whole day?"

The king and queen gave their consent. So Savitri went with Satyavan, smiling and laughing, though her heart was bursting with sorrow. Satyavan gaily pointed out to her the flowering trees, the peacocks, but Savitri kept her eyes on her husband's moods, for she knew that in a few hours he would be dead. They picked fruit and filled their bags with it, and then Satyavan began to chop down some branches for firewood. All at once he came to his wife, crying,

"Oh, my head aches! I feel like it is shot through with a thousand darts! I have to lie down; I'm so weak I can't even stand."

Savitri helped Satyavan to lie down, and she took his head in her lap. He fell asleep at once. Savitri looked up, to see a man dressed in red approaching through the trees. He was huge and dark, though his body burned like the sun. His eyes were red, he wore a jeweled crown on his head and carried a noose in his hand, and he was dreadful to behold. Seeing him, Savitri gently lay her husband's head on the ground and stood up. With trembling heart she said,

"Sire, I take you for some god. Who are you, and what do you intend to do?"

The figure replied,

"You are strong-willed and full of ascetic merit if you can see me, child, and so I will answer you. I am Yama, Lord of the Dead. Your husband's days have run out, and now I am going to bind him in this noose and take him away with me."

With this, Yama pulled out with his noose a person the size of a thumb from Satyavan's body. When Satyavan's life had thus been taken away, the body lost its breath and color, and it became unsightly. Yama held onto Satyavan's soul and began to walk toward the south. Savitri followed after him.

"Go back, Savitri," said Yama, "and perform funeral rites for your husband. He is dead."

But Savitri followed along and talked with the Lord of the Dead. After a while, Yama said to her,

"Savitri, your words and manner please me. Ask a boon from me. Except for the life of your husband, I will grant anything you ask."

Savitri said, "My father-in-law Dumatsena has lost his sight. Grant, Lord Yama, that his sight be returned to him."

"It is granted," said Yama. "Now return home."

But Savitri continued along with him, and she continued to talk. Again Yama was pleased by what she said, and again he told her to ask a boon, except for the life of Satyavan.

"Grant then," said Savitri, "that my father-in-law's kingdom be restored to him and that he continue for many years to rule it happily and well."

"It is granted," said Yama. "And now you must return home. Go back."

But Savitri kept following along behind, and at last the Lord of the Dead said to her,

"Ask one more boon, but then go back. This time, ask something for yourself, anything but the return of your husband."

"Then," said Savitri, "I ask that many sons be born to me."

"It is granted," said Yama. "Now go back."

Savitri stood where she was. "Lord Yama," she said, "a Hindu woman can marry only once."

The Lord of the Dead saw what he had done, and for a moment he hesitated. Then he untied the noose from around Satyavan's soul and with a glad heart said to Savitri,

"There, child, your husband is set free. O brave and virtuous one, in such a way do the gods love to be defeated by mortals."

Savitri returned to where the ash-colored corpse of Satyavan lay. She took his head on her lap once more and waited. In a few moments, her husband's life and color returned, and he awoke.

"How long I've slept," he said. "I dreamed I was in some foreign land, and that a dark flaming man was dragging me away."

"That was no dream," said Savitri. "But it is night now, and the jackals are howling throughout the forest. Your parents will be worried. Let's go home, and then I'll tell you what happened."

She helped Satyavan to his feet, and together they made their way back through the dark woods. When they reached home, Savitri recounted what had occurred, and indeed, everything the Lord of the Dead had granted came to pass.

The Mad Priest

A certain mad priest, whose name nobody remembers, lived in a temple in the hills. He would sing or he would cry for no apparent reason; once somebody saw him boiling a stone for his supper.

On the ninth of September an official of the district went up to the mountain for a picnic, riding in his sedan chair and followed by attendants with official red umbrellas.

After lunch the official was walking by the temple and had hardly reached the front door, when out rushed the priest, barefooted and ragged, holding a yellow umbrella. He opened the umbrella and raised it over the official's head, crying out like one of the attendants, "Make way! Make way!" Then he drew himself right up to the official's face and burst into giggles. The official was furious. "Take him away! Get rid of him!" he yelled to his attendants.

The priest fled. The attendants all chased after him. Suddenly the priest turned around and threw down his umbrella, which broke into pieces; the pieces all turned into falcons which flew about in all directions. The umbrella handle turned into a huge serpent, with red scales and glaring eyes, and it slithered toward the men. All of them would have dashed off, but one of the attendants stopped them. "It's only an illusion that the priest made up with his magic," he told them. "It can't hurt us at all."

The man seized a knife and rushed at the snake, which thereupon opened its mouth and swallowed him whole. The others were terrified. They picked up the official and fled away with him in the chair, not stopping for breath until they had run more than a mile down the mountain.

When they had recovered from their fright, several of the attendants were so worried about their friend that they crept back up the hill to see what had become of him. No sign of the snake. No priest. No attendant.

But from a hollow old ash tree just to their left, they heard peculiar sounds, as if there were a donkey inside, wheezing. At first they were afraid to go near, then they cautiously tiptoed over and peeped into a hole in the trunk. There jammed in tight, with his feet in the air, was the foolish attacker of the serpent.

Since it was impossible to drag him out, they immediately began to chop down the tree, but by the time they got him out, he was unconscious. After many hours, he came to himself again, and was carried home.

The temple still stands in the hills, and they say that new shoots are pushing out from the stump of the hollow ash, but the priest has never been heard of again.

The Buried Moon

Long ago, the land of Carrs was all bogs and marsh, with great pools of black water between the mools and hummocks. The Moon shone just as she does now, and when she shone she lighted up the bogpools, so that one could walk about almost as safely as in the day.

But when she didn't shine, out came the things that dwelled in the darkness and went about seeking to do evil and harm; Quicks and Bogles and Crawling Horrors, all came out when the Moon didn't shine.

The Moon heard of this and was troubled. "I'll see for myself, I will," said she. "Maybe it's not so bad as folks make out."

Sure enough, at the month's end down she stepped, wrapped in a black cloak, and a black hood over her yellow shining hair. Straight she went to the bog edge and looked about her; water here and water there; waving tussocks and trembling mools, and great black

snags all twisted and bent. Before her all was dark —
dark but for the glimmer of the stars in the pools and the
light that came from her own white feet stealing out of
her black cloak.

The Moon drew her cloak tighter about and
trembled, but she wouldn't go back without seeing all
there was to be seen; so on she went, stepping as lightly
as the wind in summer from tuft to tuft between the
greedy gurgling waterholes. Just as she came near a
big black pool, her foot slipped and she almost tumbled
in. She grabbed with both hands at a snag nearby to
steady herself, but as she touched it, it twined itself
around her wrists like a pair of handcuffs and gripped
her so that she couldn't move. She pulled and twisted
and fought, but it was no good. She was held fast and
would stay held fast.

Presently as she stood trembling in the dark, won-
dering if help would come, she heard something calling
in the distance — calling, calling, and then dying away
with a sob, till the marshes were full of this pitiful
crying sound. Then she heard steps floundering along,
squishing in the mud and slipping on the tufts, and
through the darkness she saw a white face with great
fear-filled eyes.

It was a man who had strayed in the bogs. Crazed
with fear he struggled on toward the flickering light that

looked like help and safety. And when the poor Moon saw that he was coming nearer and nearer to the deep hole, further and further from the path, she was so mad and so sorry that she struggled and fought and pulled harder than ever. And though she couldn't get loose, she twisted and turned until her black hood fell back off her shining yellow hair, and the beautiful light that came from it drove away the darkness.

Oh, but the man cried with joy to see the light again. At once all the Evil Things fled back into the dark corners, for they cannot abide light. Now he could see where he was and where the path was, and how he could get out of the marsh. He was in such haste to get away from the Quicks and Bogles and Horrors that dwelled there that he scarcely looked at the brave light that came from the beautiful shining yellow hair, streaming out over the black cloak and falling to the water at his feet. The Moon herself was so taken up with saving him and with rejoicing that he was back on the right path that she clean forgot that she needed help herself and that she was held fast by the black snag.

So off he went, spent and gasping, and stumbling and sobbing with joy, fleeing for his life out of the terrible bogs. Then it occurred to the Moon that she would like to go with him. She pulled and fought as if she were mad till, spent with tugging, she fell on her knees at the

foot of the snag and the black hood fell forward over her head. So out went the blessed light and back came the darkness, with all its Evil Things, with a screech and a howl. They came crowding around her, mocking and snatching and beating, shrieking with rage and spite, and swearing and snarling, for they knew her for their old enemy who drove them back into the corners and kept them from working their wicked wills.

"Drat thee!" yelled the witch-bodies, "thou'st spoiled our spells this year agone!"

"And us thou sent'st to brood in the corners!" howled the Bogles.

All the other Evil Things joined in till the very tussocks shook and the water gurgled. Then they fought and squabbled about what they should do with her till a pale gray light began to come in the sky. When the creatures saw that, they were afraid they might not have time to work their will, and they caught hold of the Moon and laid her deep in the water at the foot of the snag. The Bogles fetched a strange big stone and rolled it on top of her to keep her from rising, and they told two of the Will-o'-the-Wisps to take turns watching on the black snag, to see that she lay safe and still.

The days passed, and it was the time for the new Moon to rise, and the folk put pennies in their pockets and straws in their caps so as to be ready for her. The

Moon was a good friend to the marsh folk, and they were glad when the dark time was gone, the paths were safe again, and the Evil Things were driven back by the blessed light into the darkness and the waterholes.

But days and days passed and the new Moon never came. The nights were dark and the Evil Things were worse than ever. Still the days went on and the new Moon never came. Naturally the poor folk were strangely fearful, and many of them went to the Wise Woman who lived in the old mill to ask her if she could find out where the Moon had gone.

"Well," she said, after looking in the brewpot and in the mirror and in the Book, "it's mighty queer, but I can't rightly tell ye what's happened to her. If ye hear of aught, come and tell me."

So they went their ways, and as days went by and never a Moon came, naturally they talked and wondered—at home and at the inn, and in the garth. One day, as they sat on the great settle in the inn, a man from the far end of the boglands was smoking and listening, when all at once he sat up and slapped his knee. "My faicks!" said he, "I'd clean forgot, but I reckon I kens where the Moon be!" He told of how he was lost in the bogs, and how, when he was nearly dead with fright, the light shone out, and he found the path and got home safe.

So off they all went to the Wise Woman and told her about it, and she looked in the pot and the Book again, and then she nodded her head. "It's dark still, childer, dark," said she, "and I can't rightly see, but do as I tell ye, and ye'll find out for yourselves. Go all of ye, just afore the night gathers, put a stone in your mouth, and take a hazel twig in your hand, and say never a word till you're safe home again. Then walk on and fear not, far into the midst of the marsh, till ye find a coffin, a candle, and a cross. Then ye'll not be far from your Moon; look, and m'appen ye'll find her!"

The next night at twilight, out they went together, every one with a stone in his mouth and a hazel twig in his hand, and feeling fearful and creepy. They stumbled and stottered along the paths into the midst of the bogs; they saw nought, though they heard sighings and flutterings in their ears and felt cold wet fingers touching them. Looking around for the coffin, the candle, and the cross, they came at last to the pool beside the great snag where the Moon lay buried. All at once they stopped, quaking and trembling, for there was the great stone, half in, half out of the water, for all the world like a strange big coffin, and at the head was the black snag, stretching out its two arms in a dark gruesome cross, and on it a dim light flickered like a dying candle. They all knelt down in the mud and said "Our

Lord," first forward, because of the cross, and then backward, to keep off the Bogles, but without speaking out, for they knew that the Evil Things would catch them if they didn't do as the Wise Woman had told them.

Then they went nearer and took hold of the big stone and shoved it up. Afterwards they said that for one short moment they saw a strange and beautiful face looking up at them glad-like out of the black water; but the light came so quick and so white and shining that they stepped back blinded, and the very next minute, when they could see again, there was the full Moon in the sky, bright and beautiful as ever, shining down at them, making the bogs and the paths as clear as day, and stealing into the very corners, as though she'd have driven the darkness and the Bogles clean away if she could.

The illustrations for *The Buried Moon and other stories* were done on bogus paper, a gray, coarse, very heavy and very cheap newsprint. For the most part, the illustrations were painted with a brush in India ink and white tempera; occasionally pencil, ballpoint pen, wet and dry wadded Kleenex dipped in ink or water, cut-out paper, crayon and felt markers were used. Most of the originals were painted to size, although some were larger. Very few of the pictures were "imagined"; the people, animals, buildings, trees and such were almost always drawn from life.